PUBLIC LIBRARY
W9-BXG-994

This epic quest
belongs to

For Mum, Dad, Sarah,
and epic-quest enthusiasts everywhere.

Copyright © 2015 by Matty Long

All rights reserved. Published by Scholastic Press, an imprint of Scholastic Inc.,
Publishers since 1920. SCHOLASTIC, SCHOLASTIC PRESS, and associated logos are
trademarks and/or registered trademarks of Scholastic Inc.

Super Happy Magic Forest was originally published in the United Kingdom
by Oxford University Press Children's Books in 2015.

The publisher does not have any control over and does not assume
any responsibility for author or third-party websites or their content.

No part of this publication may be reproduced, stored in a retrieval system,
or transmitted in any form or by any means, electronic, mechanical,
photocopying, recording, or otherwise, without written permission of the publisher.
For information regarding permission, write to Scholastic Inc., Attention:
Permissions Department, 557 Broadway, New York, NY 10012.

This book is a work of fiction. Names, characters, places, and incidents are either
the product of the author's imagination or are used fictitiously,
and any resemblance to actual persons, living or dead, business
establishments, events, or locales is entirely coincidental.

Library of Congress Cataloging-in-Publication Data available

ISBN 978-0-545-86059-8

10 9 8 7 6 5 4 3 2 1   16 17 18 19 20

Printed in China   62
First American edition, March 2016

SUPER HAPPY MAGIC FOREST

BY MATTY LONG

Scholastic Press · New York

This story begins in the Super Happy Magic Forest, where everybody enjoys picnics, fun, and dancing all year round. This is all because of the Mystical Crystals of Life.

BUTTERFLY HORSE

MYSTICAL CRYSTALS OF LIFE

LOLLIPOP POND

MAGIC STONES

DANCING FIELDS

BEST FISHING POND

But the forces of evil were at work. One day,
the Mystical Crystals of Life were

STOLEN.

Old Oak, the wisest in all the Super Happy Magic Forest, called an urgent meeting.

Five heroes were chosen. Everybody agreed that
they were the bravest warriors in all the land.

With barely enough time to pack a lunch,
the heroes began their epic quest.

They showed great courage in the face of grave danger.

The heroes stopped for a picnic,
but they were attacked!

They decided to pack up and continue their
epic quest to Goblin Tower.

At last our heroes arrived at the very
doorstep of evil: Goblin Tower. The fate
of the Super Happy Magic Forest was
in their hands . . . and hooves.

They returned to the Super Happy Magic Forest,
where the true evil revealed himself.